Scout's Honor

by Erica David

Illustrated by Ron Zalme

SCHOLASTIC INC.

New York   Toronto   London   Auckland   Sydney
Mexico City   New Delhi   Hong Kong   Buenos Aires

Chapters

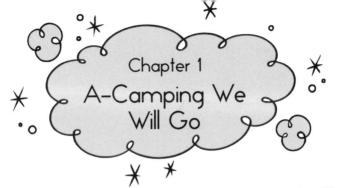

Chapter 1
A-Camping We Will Go

"I love Squirrely Scout camping trips!"
Timmy Turner said to his friends Chester
and A.J.

"Nature rocks!" Chester exclaimed.

"It's so natural!" A.J. added.

Little did they know that something unnatural was waiting for them just around the bend.

"Troop, meet your new leader, Remy
Buxaplenty!" the scoutmaster announced.

"I prefer *Master Supreme Commander,*"
Remy said.

"What the heck?" Timmy whispered.

"Now that I'm in charge," Remy began, "there are some new rules. First, the Squirrely Scouts will now be called the Remy Scouts."

"No way!" Timmy muttered.

"Second, as Remy Scouts, you're here to serve me and ONLY ME! Any questions?" asked Remy, waving a large wad of cash in front of them.

Timmy ducked behind a bush to call his fairy godparents.

"Cosmo! Wanda!" Timmy cried. "It's that rich kid who lost his godparent in a magical duel with us."

14

"That's right, Timmy," replied Wanda.
"But according to *Da Rules,* Remy
Buxaplenty won't remember ever having a
godparent—even Juandissimo Magnifico."

"You promised never to say that name again!" Cosmo whined.

"What name?" asked Wanda. "Juandissimo Magnifico? Juandissimo Magni—"

"—La, la, la! I can't hear you!" Cosmo shouted.

"Oooo, Cosmo. You're so cute when you're jealous!" teased Wanda.

"Guys!" Timmy interrupted. "Remy's at it again—using his money to buy everything. We have to show him that the Squirrely Scouts aren't for sale!"

Chapter 2
Troop for Sale

"Can you believe this Buxaplenty kid?"
Timmy asked Chester. "He thinks he can
get us to do anything just for money."

"Yeah," said Chester. "The nerve of him."

"He acts like we've never seen a dollar before," Timmy complained.

"Um, yeah," Chester agreed.

"What are you doing?" Timmy cried.

"Sorry, Timmy, but money is money," Chester explained.

"I can't believe this!" said Timmy.

"What's not to believe?" Remy sneered. "What Remy wants, Remy gets."

"I gotta find A.J.," Timmy thought. "He's too smart to be bought."

A little later, Timmy found A.J. by the
lake. "Remy's out of control!" he exclaimed.
"You have to help me stop him!"

"I think you're overreacting," A.J. replied.

"Overreacting? He's trying to buy us!" Timmy shouted.

Timmy and A.J. walked back into the
camp together.

"Fish for you, O Great One," A.J. said
to Remy.

"Not you, too!" Timmy wailed.

"Sorry," A.J. said, shrugging. "Blame it
on the economy."

"I guess I'm on my own then,"
muttered Timmy.

Chapter 3
May the Best Scout Win

That evening, Timmy barged into

Remy's tent.

"Listen up, Buxaplenty! You can't just go around buying people!" Timmy yelled.

"Oh?" Remy snickered.

"That's right. The Squirrely Scouts aren't for sale!" declared Timmy.

"Five hundred bucks says they are," Remy argued.

"Don't you get it? There are some things money can't buy like . . . like the Badger Badge!" said Timmy.

"The Badger Badge?" Remy asked.

"Yeah," Timmy replied. "It's only awarded to those who complete three tests of true scoutsmanship."

"What sort of tests?" said Remy, skeptically.

"Well, first you swim across the lake. Then you have to photograph the rare Dimmsdale daisy. Last, you have to climb Mt. Dimmsdale," Timmy explained.

"That's easy. I can do that,"
Remy bragged.

"Without money?" asked Timmy.

"Of course!" Remy snapped.

"All right, it's a challenge then. The first person to finish all three tasks wins control of the scouts. No money allowed," Timmy told him.

"Fine," Remy agreed.

"And the loser waits on the troop hand and foot for the rest of the trip," added Timmy.

"Deal," Remy said. "Prepare to lose, Turner!"

Chapter 4
The Badger Badge

The next morning, Timmy and Remy
began their contest for the Badger Badge.
"Empty those pockets, Buxaplenty!"
Timmy demanded.

"Relax, Turner, my pockets are empty.

Scared?" taunted Remy.

"In your dreams!" Timmy shot back.

"On your mark, get set, GO!" A.J. said.

Timmy and Remy dove into the lake.

After a few minutes of swimming, Timmy
was already getting tired.

"Wanda! Cosmo!" he called. "I wish I
could swim like a fish!"

"Sorry, Timmy, no can do," Wanda said.

"What do you mean?" Timmy asked.

"That would be cheating," replied Cosmo.

"You told Remy no magic allowed."

"No, I didn't," Timmy argued. "I said no
money!"

"Well, money is all the magic Remy has,"
Wanda explained.

"Yeah," Cosmo chimed in. "He sure cast a spell on your troop."

"But this stinks!" Timmy cried.

"Cheer up," Wanda said, brightly. "You can do it!"

Meanwhile, Remy used his own special
brand of magic.

"To shore, Fenwick!" he commanded.

Back on land, A.J. announced the results.

"Round one goes to Remy," he said.

"What's the matter, Turner? Tired?"
Remy teased.

Timmy glared at him.

After a short rest and a change of clothes, Timmy was ready for the second challenge. "Remy's up to something," he muttered. "You two disguise yourselves and keep an eye on him. I've gotta find the Dimmsdale daisy first!"

In another part of the woods, Remy was just as busy. "Can you ship it to me this afternoon?" he asked.

"That'll be expensive," answered the shopkeeper.

"Money is no object," Remy assured her. "Now, here's my credit card number . . ."

Timmy and Remy returned to camp with their photos at the same time.

"You both win this one," A.J. said.

"Though Remy's photo is far superior."

The contest continued.
"Know . . . Remy's . . .
cheating," Timmy huffed.
"Must . . . reach . . .
top . . . first."

When Timmy reached the top of Mt. Dimmsdale, Remy was waiting for him.

"Well, Turner," Remy gloated,
"it looks like you've lost."

49

Chapter 5
Of Scouts and S'mores

"You cheated!" Timmy shouted.

"Oh, yeah? Prove it," Remy said, smugly.

Just then Cosmo and Wanda pounced
on Remy.

"Down, beasts!" Remy yelled. Several
pieces of paper dropped from Remy's
pants pockets.

"Hey, those are receipts!" Timmy cried.
"You've been using money. I knew it!"

"These friendly woodland creatures have shown us the truth," A.J. exclaimed. "Remy, you lose."

"No!" screamed Remy. "I never lose! I'm too rich to lose!"

"Anyone can lose," Timmy said. "But it takes a true Squirrely Scout to win."

RECEIPT

That evening, the Squirrely Scouts gathered around the campfire to celebrate their freedom and Timmy's Badger Badge.

54

"Pal, will you forgive us for serving Remy?" Chester asked.

"Sure," Timmy replied. "It's not easy to resist the power of money."

"I don't know what came over me," said the scoutmaster. "It was almost like . . . like . . ."

"Magic?" Timmy suggested.

"Yes," the scoutmaster answered. "Like magic."

Timmy smiled as a cute squirrel and a funny-looking beaver darted across the clearing.

"Guys, I'll be right back," he said to the Squirrely Scouts.

"We're proud of you, Timmy,"
Wanda exclaimed.

"You got that Badger Badge all on your
own!" Cosmo congratulated him.

"But if you two hadn't helped prove Remy was cheating, I would have lost," Timmy replied.

"We're a great team," Wanda said.

"I know," Timmy agreed. "I wouldn't trade you guys for a million bucks!"